NOT-SO-IMPOSSIBLE TALES

Oliver and the Seawigs

Cakes in Space

CAKES IN SPACE

BY PHILIP REEVE
AND SARAH McINTYRE

RANDOM HOUSE 🏠 NEW YORK

Text copyright © 2014 by Philip Reeve
Cover art and interior illustrations copyright © 2014 by Sarah McIntyre

Visit us on the Web! randomhousekids.com

Educators and librarians, for a variety of teaching tools, visit us at RHTeachersLibrarians.com

Library of Congress Cataloging-in-Publication Data
Reeve, Philip, author.
Cakes in space / by Philip Reeve and Sarah McIntyre. — First American edition.
p. cm.
"Originally published by Oxford University Press in 2014"—Copyright page.
Summary: "When ten-year-old Astra and her family move to a new planet, she must save the spaceship and its crew from man-eating cakes, aliens, and more."
—Provided by publisher
ISBN 978-0-385-38792-7 (trade) — ISBN 978-0-385-38795-8 (lib. bdg.) —
ISBN 978-0-385-38794-1 (ebook)
[1. Interplanetary voyages—Fiction. 2. Space ships—Fiction.
3. Human-alien encounters—Fiction. 4. Science fiction.]
I. McIntyre, Sarah, illustrator. II. Title.
PZ7.R25576Cak 2015 [Fic]—dc23 2014000428

MANUFACTURED IN CHINA

10 9 8 7 6 5 4 3 2 1

First American Edition

FOR
AFRICA

AND

ROSANNA

ONE

The trouble with space is,
there's so much of it.

An ocean of blackness
without any shore.

A never-ending nothing.

And here, all alone in the million billion miles of midnight, is one solitary moving speck. A fragile parcel filled with sleeping people and their dreams.

A ship.

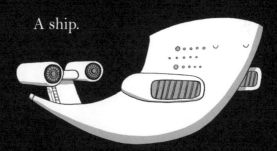

To travel from the Earth to the moon takes a few days. From Earth to Mars, a few months. To Jupiter, a few years, and to Neptune and Pluto a few years more. But Astra was traveling farther still. Much, much farther. The world called Nova Mundi, where Astra and her family were going to live, was so far from Earth that it would take them 199 years to get there.

"A HUNDRED AND NINETY-NINE YEARS ??!"

yelled Astra when her mother first told her. "We can't sit in a space-ship for one hundred and ninety-nine years! It'll be so *boring*! There won't even be anything to look at out of the window, even if spaceships *have* windows . . . which they probably don't! And I'll be *old* by the time we arrive! I'll be . . ." She counted on her fingers. "I'll be two hundred and nine years old! I'll be all wrinkly!"

But Astra's mother just laughed, bouncing Astra's baby brother, Alf, up and down on her knee until he laughed, too. "Don't worry, Astra. We won't be awake. When we go aboard the spaceship, we'll get into special sleeping pods. . . ."

"Like beds?" asked Astra.

"A little like beds," agreed her father. "And a little like freezers."

"Won't we be cold?" asked Astra with a shiver. She imagined herself snuggling down among the frozen peas and Popsicles, an ice cream cake for a pillow.

"We won't *feel* cold," said her mother. "We won't feel anything. We'll be fast asleep. The machines that run the ship will cool us right down so that we don't age. Then the ship will steer itself to Nova Mundi while we sleep, and when we get there it will wake us, and we'll feel as if only a single night has passed. And we'll be at our new home!"

"A whole new world!" said Dad.

"Nova Mundi!" said Astra.

She was excited to be going to Nova Mundi. She had seen videos and pictures of it. She and Mom and Dad and Alf were going to live in a big house there, between the wide green ocean and the fern forests, with a garden of blue grass. They would work at making the new planet ready for other people from Earth.

But she still didn't like the sound of this long, cold journey, even if she was going to be asleep.

"Will there be dreams?" she asked.

"Only nice ones," her mom promised.

And that's how it was. They took a shuttle from the spaceport.

Straight up it went, slicing through the clouds, through the sunlit air above, right up into  orbit. As it rose, the clutch of Earth's gravity grew weaker and weaker, until it slipped away entirely and Astra felt herself grow weightless. Her hands floated up off her lap; her feet kept lifting from the floor. If it hadn't been for the harness that held her in her seat, she would have drifted up and bounced off the ceiling. A few objects that the other

passengers had forgotten to secure did just that. Pens and cameras and cuddly toys went tumbling through the cabin, and the shuttle crew flew after them, graceful as swimmers in clear water, catching the lost things and returning them to their owners.

Everybody's hair started to misbehave.

"I feel sick!" complained a girl in a nearby seat, and her mother quickly passed her a bag. Astra's dad looked a little bit green, too.

"It feels like falling," he said, taking a space-sickness pill.

But Astra didn't mind the feeling. She liked it! Falling felt good, as long as she didn't have to worry about hitting

the ground. She liked the thought that they
were going to fall all the way to Nova Mundi.

The shuttle sped past the space stations that hung like chandeliers above the bright curve of the Earth, with little transport ships flitting between them.

And among all the streams and swirls of shipping was the ship that was going to carry Astra and her family to Nova Mundi.

"It's *huge!*" said Astra, eyes wide, nose pressed to the diamond glass of the porthole by her seat.

Astra had thought the shuttle she was in was big, but as it drew close to the ship, it began to seem tiny, like a little fish swimming beside a whale. It settled against the big ship's side, and there were dull, dim clangs and thuds and shudderings as it docked.

Around Astra, people began to undo their harnesses. Astra undid hers and fell straight up, rebounding off the ceiling. All around her, people were doing the same, tumbling and twirling in midair like acrobats. Children laughed and shoved themselves off the cabin's padded walls, bouncing around like Ping-Pong balls, while their parents called out to them to be careful.

By the time they had all funneled out of the shuttle and into the waiting ship, Astra was starting to get used to the idea of zero gravity. It was not like falling—more like floating in water, only without the feeling of the water around you. Her dad was still green, though.

"I thought you said we wouldn't meet any little green men," Mom said.

"Oh, very funny!" said
Dad.

"What are little green
men?" asked Astra.

23

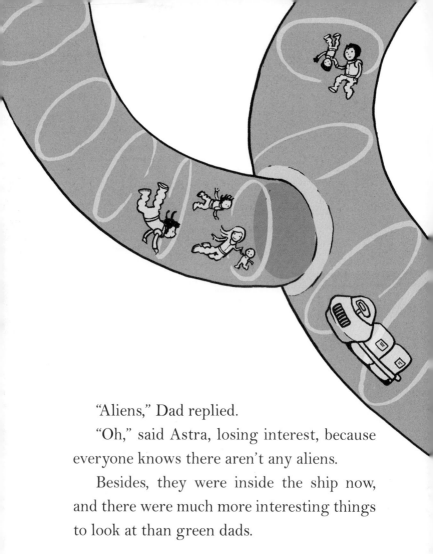

"Aliens," Dad replied.

"Oh," said Astra, losing interest, because everyone knows there aren't any aliens.

Besides, they were inside the ship now, and there were much more interesting things to look at than green dads.

The robots who would operate the ship while everybody was alseep hurried to and fro, some floating, some stomping along the corridor walls on flat magnetic feet. A floating one gathered together all the people who had just arrived and led them to a part of the ship called Hibernation Section C, where they were to spend the journey.

TWO

After that, there was a wait. A LONG wait. There were three hundred pods lining the walls of Section C—three hundred people for the fussy hibernation robots to sort out and get comfortable, which wasn't easy, with everybody floating about and children still doing Ping-Pong-ball impressions. Soon Astra started to grow hungry. She had eaten a big meal before the shuttle took off, but now an awful thought occurred to her.

It was 199 years until breakfast.

A HUNDRED AND NINETY-NINE YEARS!

Her tummy gave a hopeless gurgle. She tugged at Dad's sleeve. "Are there any cookies?"

"Just get ready for bed," said her dad.

She got ready for bed, but her tummy still felt empty. It felt as empty as all the miles and miles of space that lay between Earth and Nova Mundi—

between Astra and her breakfast.

Alf was fussing, and Mom and Dad were

both busy trying to cheer him up. Astra looked around. There were important-looking cupboards on the walls of Hibernation Section C, stenciled with words like AIR and WATER, but none of them said COOKIES. She noticed a small, roundish sort of robot pottering nearby and went over to him.

"Excuse me," she said, tapping him on his plastic back.

The robot was so startled that he whirled right around and ended up facing away from her again. Then his head swiveled around, and his camera-lens eyes peered at her.

"I am PILBEAM, at your service," he said.

"Is there anything to eat?" asked Astra. "I'm definitely peckish." ("Definitely peckish" was something that Astra's mom said sometimes. Astra thought it sounded more polite than "hungry.")

Lights flashed and flickered all over Pilbeam's spherical body. "Accessing ship's data banks," he said. And then: "There is a Nom-O-Tron 9000 Food Synthesizer located in the dining hall. Upon arrival at Nova Mundi, tasty and nutritious snacks will be provided for all passengers."

Astra didn't much like the sound of "nutritious." "Nutritious" meant "good for you," and "good for you" usually meant "vegetables." But "tasty" sounded okay, so she said, "Can I see?"

The little robot went whirring ahead of her, through a little corridor that whooshed open at the end of the big chamber and down another corridor that opened into a sort of dining hall, where clean white surfaces shone coldly in the dim light, like icebergs on an Arctic night. The lights were not turned on, because no one was expected to come in for breakfast for 199 years.

One whole wall of the big room was taken up by a huge machine, with dials and screens and lights and hatches. That seemed to be turned off, too, but when Pilbeam stuck out a little silvery arm and poked his hand into one of the hatches, it started to hum.

"Thank you, Pilbeam," said Astra.

"I am Nom-O-Tron," said the machine in a big, boomy voice, so loud that Astra was afraid her mom and dad or some of the other grown-ups would hear and come to see who was sneaking a bedtime snack.

"Shhh!" she said. "Have you got any cookies?"

"Nom-O-Tron can synthesize all foodstuffs.

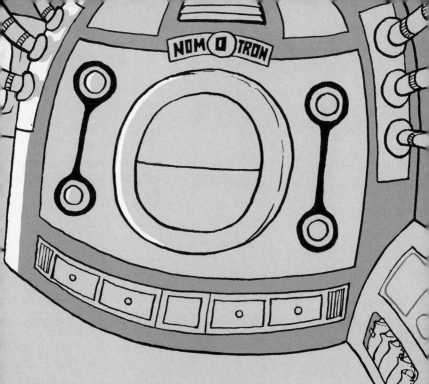

Please state the exact type of cookie you require."

"Ummm . . . a chocolate chip one?" said Astra.

Nom-O-Tron hummed a little more. Then it burbled. And it burped. In clear plastic tubes high above Astra's head, purple liquid glooped.

This is not looking hopeful, Astra thought. She had asked for a chocolate chip cookie, and the stupid machine was going to give her beet soup.

But the purple stuff was just food concentrate. There were huge tanks of it deep inside the ship, and it was the job of Nom-O-Tron to give it a shape and a flavor—whatever shape and flavor you asked for. A chocolate chip cookie, Astra had said, so it checked the ship's memory banks for chocolate chip cookies, decided on the most popular type, and set to work.

Hum, it went.

Buzz.

Spurgle.

Ping! A hatch popped open in front of Astra, and there sat a single, perfect chocolate chip cookie. She took it out and ate it. When her teeth crunched into it, crumbs flew in every direction, orbiting her head like asteroids. It was delicious.

"Wow!" she said. "Thanks, Nom-O-Tron!"

"Thanks are not necessary," replied Nom-O-Tron. It stuck out a little suction hose and sucked up the drifting crumbs, which it could recycle. "Nom-O-Tron is built to serve. Will there be anything else, miss?"

Astra didn't really feel hungry anymore, and she knew her parents would soon start to wonder where she was, but the thought that Nom-O-Tron could make any sort of food she asked for was too enticing to resist.

What would she have? A grilled cheese sandwich? No, that would take too long to eat. Another cookie? Boring!

"I know!" she said. "What about a cake? A big cake!" She was thinking that she could eat

a little now and hide the rest in her sleeping pod, in case there was a long line for breakfast when they got to Nova Mundi.

"Please state the exact type of cake you require," said Nom-O-Tron.

"A really big one!" said Astra. "And it's got to have . . ." She tried to think of all the nicest bits of cakes. Icing? Sprinkles? Creamy bits? Cakey bits? She flapped her arms about, trying to mime a cake. "Oh, just make me the most amazing, super-fantastic cake ever!" she said. "I want something brilliant! I want something so delicious, it's scary! I want the *ultimate cake*!"

Nom-O-Tron hummed.

Then it buzzed a little.

Then, quite suddenly, it shut down. Silence fell. All the lights on the front of the huge machine went off, except for a red one that flashed on and off, on and off.

Astra went closer and looked at it. The light formed a word.

WORKING

"Er . . . Nom-O-Tron?" asked Astra.

There was no reply.

"Did I break it?" she asked Pilbeam.

The little robot shrugged. Astra wouldn't have thought he could shrug, being completely round with no shoulders, but he managed it somehow.

The red light on the front of Nom-O-Tron flashed on and off, on and off.

WORKING

"I think I broke it!" said Astra nervously.

"Astra?" The door slid open, and there was

Dad. "So this is where you've got to! We've been looking for you everywhere! What are you doing in here?"

"Nothing!" said Astra quickly. "It was like this when I got here!"

Dad looked around suspiciously, but he couldn't see anything broken or out of place. He took Astra's hand and led her away. "Come on. It's bedtime!"

She waved at Pilbeam as she passed. "Good night, Pilbeam!"

"Good night, Astra," said the little robot.

THREE

The freezer beds where they were to sleep looked cold and uncomfortable at first. Astra was old enough to have a pod of her own, and she felt a bit envious of her little brother, who would sleep with their mom, curled up together as if they were in a nest.

But once Astra was tucked in under her own space duvet with Mammoth and her other cuddlies snuggled carefully in around her, she felt as if she was in a nest, too. Quite cozy.

Slowly the chattering of the other passengers fell quiet as, one by one, or family by family, the robots put them to sleep. Now Astra could hear the sounds of the ship: the humming of air pumps and computers, the slow throb of the warming-up engines like the heartbeat of a big, friendly animal. She hoped Nom-O-Tron would have mended itself by the time everyone woke up and wanted breakfast. Perhaps Pilbeam would fix it while they slept.

She looked about for Pilbeam, but she couldn't see him. Instead, a fussy robot called Bedbot drifted up to her pod and busily stuck little sensors to her arms and forehead.

"What are these for?" asked Astra.

"They will allow me to monitor you while

44

you sleep," said Bedbot. "Brain waves, heart rate . . ."

"If you have bad dreams, Bedbot will know

about it," said her dad. "She'll add more seda-tive to the air in your pod, and the bad dreams will go away."

"Okay . . . ," said Astra.

Bedbot rolled off to deal with the boy in the next pod. Astra's mom and dad hugged her.

"Sleep tight, Astra!" said Mom.

"See you on Nova Mundi, when the day is dawning!" said Dad.

"I don't feel sleepy yet!" Astra complained as the pod lid closed. Her mom and dad smiled in at her through the clear plastic. She started to worry that she wouldn't be able to get to sleep. What if everyone else went to sleep and she couldn't? What then? She yawned and said, "I don't feel even … a … little … bit …"

And then her eyes closed.

Her mom and dad watched over her until they were quite sure she was asleep. Then they went into their own pods, and soon they were sleeping, too. The lights dimmed to a faint blue glow. The pods were cooling. Frost flowers formed on the inside of their canopies.

When the ship was certain that no one was awake, it fired its engines. They pushed it away from the space station, away from the wide blue eye of Earth. It flew past the moon. It flew past Mars. It swung past the huge, striped face of Jupiter, picking up a little extra speed as the huge planet's gravity caught it and then flung it onward into the dark, into the huge, still, empty places beyond the light of the sun, while, silent in their misty rows of pods, the passengers all slept and dreamed their dreams.

And in the dining hall next to Hibernation Section C, the red light on the front of Nom-O-Tron flashed on and off, on and off:

WORKING

And then, a million billion miles from home, slap bang in the middle of nowhere at all, Astra woke up.

* * *

At first, she wasn't really sure if she was awake. She thought she might just be *dreaming* that she'd woken. She was lying with her eyes wide open, under the duvet in her freezer pod.

What a boring dream, she thought, and waited for it to end.

Instead, a cold drip landed on the tip of her nose.

Astra didn't think she could have dreamed that.

On the inside of the pod's canopy, droplets of condensation were forming. They wiggled about like glass ladybugs, confused by the lack of gravity. Now and then one would drift away from the plastic and splat on the duvet, or on Mammoth's furry head, or on Astra's face.

When they tucked her in, Mom and Dad had shown Astra the fat green button that she would press to open the canopy when the

ship reached
Nova Mundi.
"Just in case you
wake up before us," they said. That was what
must have happened, she decided. The ship
had arrived at Nova Mundi, and she was the
first one in her family to wake. Or maybe the
first on the entire ship. She listened, but she
couldn't hear any voices outside her pod.

   She found the green button and pushed it.
The lid of the pod opened with a gentle sigh.
Astra sat up.

The ship was almost in darkness. The only light came from little dim lamps set into the deck, and from the icy blue glow that shone out through the lids of all the other pods.

"Hello?" said Astra, into the shadows and the stillness.

No one answered.

Astra pushed herself out of her pod, holding Mammoth very tight. She flew to the pod where her mom was sleeping, snuggled up with baby Alf. She peeped in through the glass at them, at their calm, dreaming faces, pale behind the frost flowers. She went to Dad's pod and knocked gently on the plastic lid, but he did not stir. She drifted a little farther, peering into other pods. She saw a boy with freckles and a girl her own age who might be her friend when they reached Nova Mundi. Pushing herself gently off from walls and pillars, she floated through the whole huge hibernation compartment, drifting like

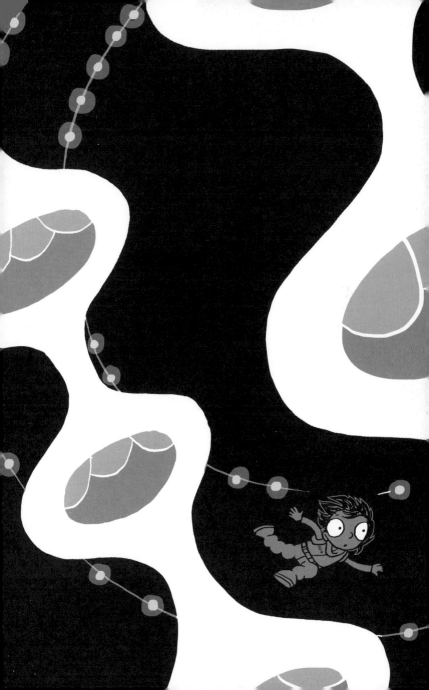

a dream above the pods, looking in at this face and that.

Everyone was fast asleep.

"Mom! Dad!" Astra shouted, banging on the lids of their pods. But they didn't stir, and there was no green button that would open the pods from the outside. There was a big red one, though. . . .

This felt like an emergency to Astra, so she pushed it. All at once, new sounds burst into the hibernation section. A siren began to honk. Astra dropped Mammoth and clapped her hands over her ears. Red lights woke like sudden rubies among the ducts and cables on the walls and started to flash. But Astra's mom and dad and all the other sleepers slept on without even stirring.

Astra waited for Bedbot to come and help her back to sleep. She caught Mammoth as he rebounded off the wall and tucked him into the waistband of her pants so she wouldn't drop him again. They waited together, afloat in the middle of Hibernation Section C.

After a while the siren and the red lights stopped, leaving an echoey silence that felt even more silent than before.

"The ship is big," Astra told Mammoth. She knew he was only a cuddly and wouldn't mind the wait, but it was comforting to hear a human voice, even if it was just her own. "It's very big. Big as a whole city, probably. Maybe Bedbot has other people to attend to. Maybe she's off in some far part of the ship. It might take her hours to get around to us. That must be it."

Her tummy rumbled, sudden and loud in the stillness. It made her remember Nom-O-Tron 9000 and the cake she had hoped to take to bed with her.

"I'm hungry," she said. "I wonder if that Nom-O-Tron has repaired itself. I wonder if it can do banana pancakes."

She went to the door that Pilbeam had

taken her through earlier. (It felt like last night to her, but actually it must have been years, decades, lifetimes ago.) The eating area was still all shadows and dim ice-sheet reflections. Nom-O-Tron was in darkness, too. Crumbs floated in the air all around Astra as she swam through that big, dark space. Far too many crumbs to have come from her eating that one chocolate chip cookie before she went to bed.

Had someone else been up, having a midnight snack?

But there was no sign of anyone, and on the front of Nom-O-Tron that single sign still flashed and flashed:

WORKING

WORKING

WORKING

There was stuff caked all around the little hatch where Astra's cookie had emerged. Some of the stuff was dry and hard and crusty, and more stuff had flowed over it and dried in its turn, and then more, building up a great fan-shaped deposit. The stuff on the surface was still sticky-looking. Astra reached out and touched it. She sniffed it. She tasted it.

"Cake mix?"

Above her head, the pipes gurgled. The purple fluids gushed and glooped. Nom-O-Tron hummed and buzzed, and suddenly—*PING!*—a cake dropped down inside the hatch.

Astra looked at the cake.

The cake looked back at Astra.

It was kind of like a cupcake, but larger, and where cupcakes sometimes had little decorative sugar flowers among the sprinkles on their icing tops, this cake had eyes.

Three of them. Little beady black ones, which glinted and blinked.

The top of the cake flipped open like a garbage-can lid, revealing a wide mouth and lots of shiny little teeth.

Astra turned to run, her legs windmilling uselessly in midair until she remembered there was no gravity.

She reached out with one foot and pushed herself off from Nom-O-Tron, just as the angry cupcake somehow sprang out of the hatch. It tumbled past her as she zoomed away.

"RAWR!"

"Aaaaaargh!"

She floated toward the door, but not fast enough; the cake was moving faster. For an awful moment she saw it rushing toward her, its top open wide to bare all its teeth. Then, out of the shadows above, something giant and sugar pink came rushing. Astra glimpsed *another* cakey mouth opening wide; there was a

GLOMP

and the cupcake was gone. The giant cake that had just eaten it went hurtling past her, a trail of crumbs bobbing in its wake. Its eyes all gleamed, looking at Astra, and she knew she had to get to the door and through it before the pink cake reached the wall and came back to get her.

She wriggled and flapped like a frantic fish, and her outstretched hand found the door control. The door whooshed open. She pulled herself through and closed the door behind her, not a moment too soon. As it shut, she heard the pink cake smash into the other side of it with a great, sticky

SPLUDGE.

Then silence.

Well, at least I know now that I'm only dreaming, thought Astra. *Because honestly, girl-eating cakes? That's the last time I eat chocolate before bed. I'm ready to wake up now....*

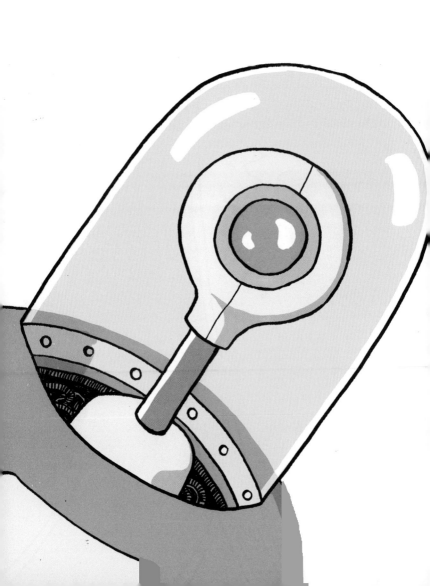

FOUR

Astra pinched herself. She pulled her nose. She hit herself so hard in the face with Mammoth that she turned a complete somersault. But she didn't wake up. This was not a dream.

When a door on the far side of the compartment opened, Astra was so startled that she did another somersault. But what came bobbing through the door was not a killer cake but a familiar little round robot.

"Pilbeam!" she shouted, waving.

The robot was so startled to see Astra floating there that his head started to turn around and around, and little red lights came on all over his body like electric measles.

"Oh, it's all right!" said Astra, trying to calm the robot down. She suddenly felt a little bit silly clutching Mammoth, so she tucked him into the waistband of her pants. "It's me! Astra!" she said helpfully. "Is your head *supposed* to keep going around like that? I mean, what if it comes unscrewed and falls off?"

The robot steadied himself. His electric eyes looked Astra up and down. "Oh my goodness!" he said. "Oh dear me! Was it you who set off the emergency alarm? You are not supposed to be awake!"

"So we aren't at Nova Mundi?"

"No, Astra."

"Are we nearly there yet?"

"No, Astra."

"When will we get there?"

"We should arrive in orbit around Nova Mundi in ninety-nine years, nine months, three weeks, six days, twelve hours, and fourteen seconds. I shall call Bedbot to get you back to sleep."

"I tried!" said Astra. "She didn't come. I think something's wrong, Pilbeam."

"There *have* been an unusual number of system failures," the robot admitted. "That is why the ship woke me."

"I think something's *really* wrong," said Astra. "There are these *cakes*!"

"Cakes?"

"They're alive! They're eating one another! One tried to eat me!"

Pilbeam's head started revolving again. He put up one hand to stop it. "I think you may have been dreaming, Astra."

"That's what I was hoping," Astra said. "But I don't think I was."

Something went drifting between them. It was a cake crumb.

Pilbeam reached out and stuck one metal finger into a wall hatch. His lights flickered in quick little patterns as he read information from the ship's computers.

"Well?" Astra asked impatiently.

"Something *is* really wrong!" said Pilbeam. "That stupid Nom-O-Tron is using up all the ship's computing power! No wonder so many faults have developed! The ship is not correcting any of the problems. It's stopped repairing itself. It hasn't checked its course for years! Nom-O-Tron is keeping it busy designing cakes!"

"Oh!" said Astra. "Oh, it's all my fault! I wasn't specific enough! If I'd asked it for a cupcake or a Swiss roll or a chocolate cake, it would have been all right, but I told it to make me something scarily delicious! I told it to make the ultimate cake!"

"It's been making batch after batch of cakes for ninety-nine years," said Pilbeam, unplugging himself from the information socket. "It's been making cakes, then scrapping them and recycling the food con-centrate and making other, more advanced cakes."

"And somehow, somewhere along the line, it made a cake that was alive!" whispered Astra.

"And they've started to evolve," said Pilbeam. "They've grown bigger and more intelligent."

"I think I asked it to make a cake that was

brilliant!" said Astra. "But I didn't mean brilliant in that way!"

"Nom-O-Tron can't have understood."

"Can't you turn it off?"

"I've tried! It won't let me."

"We have to wake somebody else up," Astra said. "Dad or the captain or some other grown-up. They'll know what to do."

"The captain is supposed to be woken as soon as the emergency alarm goes off," said Pilbeam. "She is still asleep. That system must have failed, too. In fact, all the hibernation systems are off-line. We cannot wake anyone."

From behind Astra came a familiar sound. It was the soft whoosh of a door opening, and it was as chilling as someone whispering in your ear on a dark night when you think you're all alone. Someone . . . or something . . . or some *cake* . . . had opened the door that led to the dining hall.

"Astra," said Pilbeam. His head started to

revolve again, and this time he did not try to stop it.

Astra turned her head, too—not all the way around, of course, but far enough to see the open door, and the things that had come floating through it.

They were cupcakes. There were six of them, and each was the size of a fairly large flowerpot. They hung there in formation, sprinkles bristling fiercely on their tops.

Their eyes looked like those little silver balls you get on cakes sometimes, the ones that nobody likes because they're really hard.

Actually, thought Astra, *those cupcakes look really hard, too.*

Pilbeam made a little electronic throat-clearing noise. "Astra . . ."

"Yes?" she whispered.

"Run!"

You can't really run in zero gravity, as Astra had found earlier, but there were plenty of pipes and pillars in that part of the hibernation section to pull themselves along on. Before the cupcakes could come after them, they reached the door that Pilbeam had used, shot through it, and shut it behind them. Pilbeam locked it and entered a complicated code. "That should hold them."

"But what about Mom and Dad and Alf and all the other sleepers?" asked Astra.

Pilbeam pressed another button on the control pad. A screen on the wall lit up, showing them a picture of the hibernation section. The pack of cupcakes was drifting aimlessly in midair.

"The hibernation pods are sealed shut," said Pilbeam. "They should be cake-proof. And I don't think those cakes even realize there are people in them."

Astra started to cry. She couldn't help herself. The tears squeezed out of her eyes and went wobbling away like lost raindrops. "Oh, Pilbeam!" she said. "This is all wrong! People should eat cakes, not the other way around."

Pilbeam's head revolved a few times. He wasn't sure how to deal with people crying. He tried patting her on the shoulder. "There, there, Astra," he said. "Nobody has been eaten yet, and nobody will be. We shall regain control of the ship's computer, turn off Nom-O-Tron, and vent the cakes into space."

"Can we do that?"

"I can. But I shall have to go to the main control room, at the front of the ship."

"Okay," said Astra. She remembered how big the ship had looked when she had been flying toward it in the shuttle. She thought Hibernation Section C was somewhere near the back. She expected it would take the little robot a long time to get all the way to the control room.

"Can I come with you?" she asked. "I don't want to stay here alone."

"Of course," said Pilbeam. "I don't want to go alone, either."

Astra sniffed and wiped away her tears. She took hold of one of Pilbeam's hands. Her tummy rumbled, squeakily and rather loudly.

"I'm really hungry!" she said.

"We could stop in at Hibernation Section A," said Pilbeam. "There is another Nom-O-Tron there."

"No way!" said Astra. "I'm not using one of those stupid things again! It will probably start making giant, singing waffles or evil oatmeal or something. Isn't there anything else I can eat?"

Pilbeam thought for a moment. "There is a garden just two sections from here. The ship's gardens contain over seven hundred different species of plants."

They went floating on their way.

Behind them, a strange shadow uncurled itself from the other shadows among the ducts and plumbing of the corridor wall, but they had their backs to it and did not notice.

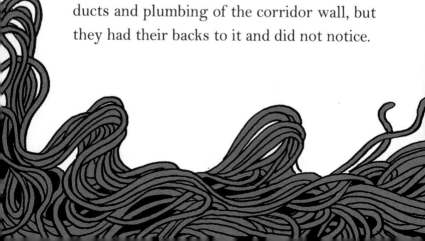

FiVE

They floated on. Each time they reached
a door, Pilbeam pressed the panel beside
it and it whirled open to let them through,
until at last one opened onto greenish
light and a smell of growing things, and

they flew through it into the garden.

Only it wasn't so much a garden as a forest. A jungle. A huge hall full of trees, the air warm and dense with mist. When the ship set off, there had been just a few saplings planted among the garden's ornamental lawns. Now they had grown into ancient giants, shaggy with moss, with branches that reached out in all directions, impossibly long and slender in the absence of gravity. New trees had grown up among them. Ivy and lichen drifted in great green clouds above the paths and twined around the few bits of ship that were still visible.

"I don't think it's meant to look like this," said Astra.

Pilbeam gave a little robot shrug. "I have never been into this section of the ship before, Astra." He held up a twig. "Breakfast?"

"I can't eat that!"

Pilbeam looked disappointed. His head

drooped, and his lights fluttered lilac and blue. "It is organic material," he said. "Humans eat organic material."

"Not like that! It usually gets turned into bread or cereal or something first. Or cookies," she added, a little wistfully.

Pilbeam looked at the twig curiously. "How do we turn it into bread-or-cereal?"

"I'm not sure. . . ."

Astra went exploring, through a hollowed-out tree trunk and into the heart of the garden. She could almost have been in a great forest back on Earth, except that she was flying between the trees instead of walking, and when she looked up, she did not see the sun but the glare of big lamps, slowly dimming as the garden's artificial day turned to artificial night. She hoped she could find something to eat before it grew completely dark. For a moment she was afraid that there might be wild animals lurking among the trees, but then she remembered that there were no animals on board the ship. No insects, either—the ship could not have bugs swarming everywhere, creeping into all its complicated workings. These things that buzzed like gnats around Astra's head were flying robots, e-bugs, buzzing from flower to flower with cargoes of pollen. Down in the soft layers of leaf mold beneath her, e-beetles would be at work—mechanical munching machines, busy breaking down the dead wood and fallen leaves.

Astra followed a flight of gossamer-winged e-bugs and found what she had been hoping for: a fruit tree.

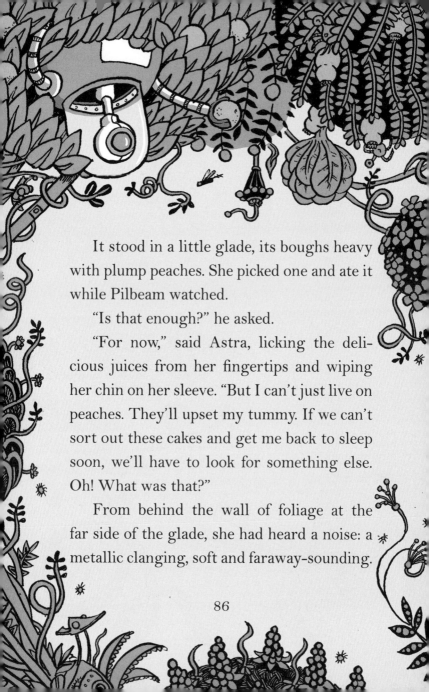

It stood in a little glade, its boughs heavy with plump peaches. She picked one and ate it while Pilbeam watched.

"Is that enough?" he asked.

"For now," said Astra, licking the delicious juices from her fingertips and wiping her chin on her sleeve. "But I can't just live on peaches. They'll upset my tummy. If we can't sort out these cakes and get me back to sleep soon, we'll have to look for something else. Oh! What was that?"

From behind the wall of foliage at the far side of the glade, she had heard a noise: a metallic clanging, soft and faraway-sounding.

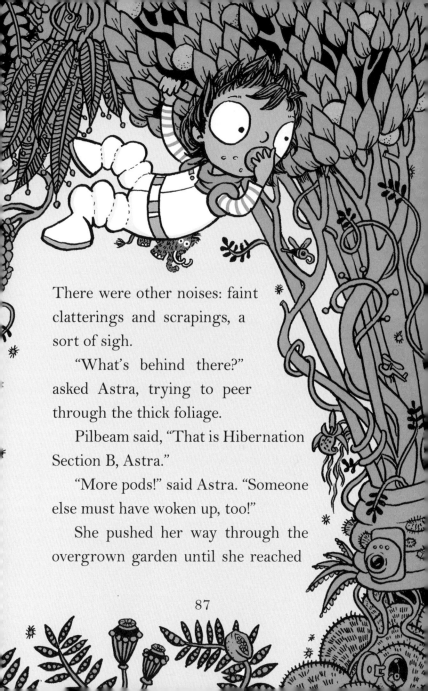

There were other noises: faint clatterings and scrapings, a sort of sigh.

"What's behind there?" asked Astra, trying to peer through the thick foliage.

Pilbeam said, "That is Hibernation Section B, Astra."

"More pods!" said Astra. "Someone else must have woken up, too!"

She pushed her way through the overgrown garden until she reached

a big door, on which a letter B could still be seen beneath the moss. She opened it, hoping that the someone who had woken up in there would be a grown-up who could tell her what to do.

"Hello?" she called into the dim blue shade of a hibernation section just like the one she'd woken in. Astra peered into the nearest pod. A mother with two tiny children lay sleeping there. Astra moved on, looking into pod after pod. Everyone was asleep.

From somewhere beyond the compartment came those noises again: clangs and hammerings, work sounds.

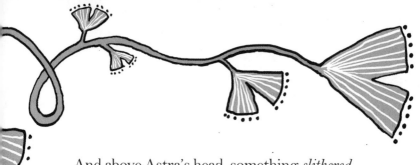

And above Astra's head, something *slithered*.

She looked up, past the tiers of gently glowing pods to where there were pipes and ducts and tangles of striped spaghetti plumbing. Something clung there in the shadows. Something lay pooled among the pipes like soup. Ripples of light ran over it as it moved. It looked like spilled oil as it moved between the pipes, but it stretched like something with muscles. Dark tentacles stretched thoughtfully toward Astra like wet black ropes, then withdrew again.

Astra had forgotten to breathe. She gulped some air in with a great gasp and said, "Pilbeam?"

"Yes, Astra?"

"Let's get out of here!"

"Yes, Astra!"

There was a door nearby. It was not the door that they'd come in by, but Astra didn't care. She kicked herself off the nearest pod lid as hard as she could and shot through the compartment like a missile. Pilbeam zipped ahead of her and opened the door. She grabbed the edges of it and fumbled through, imagining that black thing behind her, reaching out its oily strands, its hungry tentacles.

"Shut the door! Shut the door!"

"Yes, Astra."

"Lock it!"

"It is locked, Astra."

"Nail wobbly bits of wood across it! Shove a cupboard against it!"

"I do not have any wobbly bits of wood, Astra. And what is a cupboard?"

"Never mind."

Astra kicked herself along yards and yards of corridor, needing to put as much distance as she could between herself and the whatever-it-was.

"Pilbeam?"

"Yes, Astra?"

"What was that? Was it a cake?"

"I don't think so, Astra."

"Then . . . was it a monster?"

Pilbeam's head went around a couple of times. Lights

blinked on and off all over him. "There are no monsters listed among the ship's crew, passengers, or cargo," he said.

"Then it must have come from outside!" said Astra. "It must be some sort of *alien*!"

A breeze plucked at Astra's sleeve. Cool air blew on her face, and she lifted her head and let it stir her hair. It was refreshing, blowing along that stale and stuffy corridor. But Pilbeam said, "Oh no! Oh dear!"

"What?"

The robot went whizzing off, calling for Astra to follow him. It would have been hard not to, for the breeze she'd felt was rising to a gale, buffeting her after him along the corridor. He came to a locker and opened it. Inside hung six spacesuits, starting to stir and twitch and dance as the wind's fingers found them.

"Put this on!" said Pilbeam, finding the one that was nearest to Astra's size and unzipping it. It flapped like a flag as she fought her way into it. It was too big for her, but she was glad of that, because it meant that there was room inside for Mammoth, too. The wind was howling now; the long corridor hooted like a flute. Then Pilbeam fitted the bubble-shaped helmet over her head and the sounds of the ship grew faraway and watery. Astra could still hear Pilbeam, though, loud and clear through the helmet's radio.

"The hull must have been damaged. The ship is venting air into space."

"But if all the air vents into space, what will every-body breathe?"

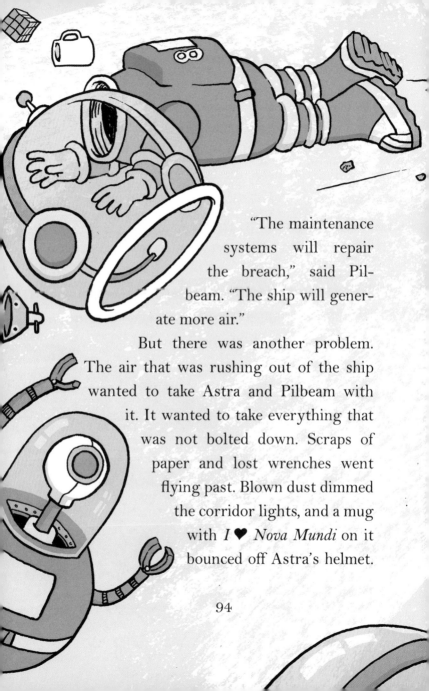

"The maintenance systems will repair the breach," said Pilbeam. "The ship will generate more air."

But there was another problem. The air that was rushing out of the ship wanted to take Astra and Pilbeam with it. It wanted to take everything that was not bolted down. Scraps of paper and lost wrenches went flying past. Blown dust dimmed the corridor lights, and a mug with *I* ♥ *Nova Mundi* on it bounced off Astra's helmet.

The empty spacesuits jittered on their hangers as the wind rose, as if they were all eager to join the fun. The spare helmets jostled against each other with glassy creaks and squeaks. One by one, the suits took flight and the wind whirled them off around the bend of the corridor and away. When they were all gone, it seemed to turn its attention to Astra. She felt her fingers being pried from the bulkhead she was clinging to.

"Hold on, Astra!" pleaded Pilbeam. But the wind snatched her up and carried her joyously away. She bounced off bulkheads, snatched at passing pillars, once grabbed hold of a control panel that anchored her for a few breathless seconds before its fixings gave way. Sparks skittered as it tore from the wall, and the wind wrenched the control panel out of her hands as she went hurtling on her way. "Pilbeeeeeeeeeeeam!" she screamed as she was bounced and bundled on alone through the maze of corridors, part of a growing cloud of tools and litter all headed in the same direction. His voice crackled at her for a moment over her helmet radio: "Don't worry, Astra! You have a spacesuit! I'll come and find you!"

But what good will a spacesuit be? thought Astra. *I'll be lost in space! How will I ever get back aboard the ship?*

She was hurtling through the ship's outer sections now, through docking bays where shuttle craft stood waiting. Fuel drums and hoses and more empty spacesuits were caught up in the crazy whirlwind and funneled toward one of the ship's big docking hatches.

In the middle of the hatch, a circular hole had appeared. It was so neat around the edges that Astra didn't think it could be natural, but before she could even start to wonder who would have cut a hole in the hatch and how, she was sucked through it.

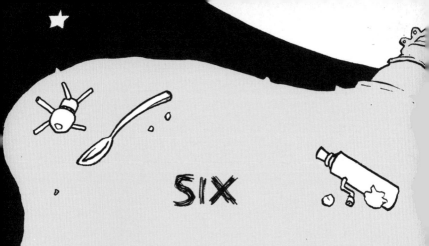

SIX

She expected to find herself out in the endless dark, with nothing to see but the spilled-salt glitter of the stars and the spreading cloud of lost stuff twinkling as it exploded away from the ship.

Instead, she was in a kind of bag.

It was a big bag, but it was already so full of things that had been sucked out of the ship that it was quite hard to move without bumping into something—a switched-off robot, or a tumbling packing crate. Slowly the currents that swirled through the bag brought her close to its side. It was made of transparent stuff, and she could see out through it.

The ship was below her. And above her was *another* ship: a grimy, lumpy, grungy, chunky, mechanical muddle of a ship, covered with mysterious stencilings that might have been letters or numbers, bristling with prongs and antennas and little blister windows. The bag in which Astra was trapped was attached to a big nozzle on the side of it.

"Hey!" she shouted, smacking her gloved hands against the sides of the bag. It was taut, but it yielded slightly, like a big sheet of rubber. She kicked and punched at it, until a finger of light came sweeping across the outside of the bag and dazzled her. It was a searchlight, mounted on the strange spaceship. "Stop it!" Astra shouted. "You're sucking everything out of our ship!"

The light kept shining on her. She shielded her eyes with her hand. Something moved on the outside of the bag. For a moment,

bedazzled, she was afraid it was another tentacly black oil-spill thing, but it was not. It
was a monster, all right, but a different sort
of monster: a squat, plump one in a grease-
stained spacesuit like a grubby chimney pot,
with a nest of eyes on stalks poking out of his
helmet.

"Ploogah stoofie!" shouted the creature,
his voice loud and buzzy on her helmet radio.
"Brixit! Floop!"

"I'm sorry," said Astra. "I don't understand. . . ."

"Quindaboody! Flarpo! Skudge!" the creature shouted. But he wasn't talking to Astra
now; he'd turned to look up at his spaceship
and was gesturing with all three arms to
another of his kind, in one of those bubble
windows.

A roaring noise so big that Astra hadn't
even noticed it fell suddenly silent. The
engine that had been pulling air and junk and

Astra out of the hole in the ship's hatch was switched off. The eddies of stuff in the bag eddied slower. Astra went with them, drifting away from the bag's side, out of the light, out of sight of the creature outside. But soon, through the tumbling flotsam and the shifting shadows, the creature came looking for her, puttering along on a little vehicle like a flying scooter, with two more just like him clinging to the back.

"Ploogah stoofie!" he said, seeing Astra floating there. "Bimnitts! Strim-awoogah!"

Astra remembered her mom and dad telling her that there were no such things as aliens. But then they'd probably thought there were no such things as man-eating cupcakes, either. She was going to have lots to tell them if they ever woke up.

The alien brought his scooter to a stop in front of her. "Flooba prunto!" he said.

"Brixit!" agreed one of his friends, gesturing at Astra with a thing that might have been a space gun, or possibly a space plunger. "Crumpi!"

"I don't understand!" shouted Astra, waving her hands about in an "I don't understand" sort of way.

The first alien looked down and twiddled one of the dials on the front of his dirty spacesuit. Or was it a her? It was hard to tell, but he seemed sort of bossy, so Astra decided he must be a boy. "Flimbu? Snarka floodi . . . Poogo! Ah, that's more like it. . . ." His crown of eyeballs turned to her again. "Now, what are you doing in our collecting bag? Are you danger- ous? If you try and make trouble, Ploodle here will zap you with her Arkle-splifflicator!"

Astra looked nervously down the hole at the front of the plunger thing, which the second alien was still pointing at her threateningly. The first alien's suit might not have been able to find a translation for "Arkle-splifflicator," but Astra still felt pretty sure that she didn't want her arkles splifflicated: the last things she needed now, she felt, were splifflicated arkles. She put her hands up.

"I didn't mean to end up in your bag," she said. "But what do you expect if you start making holes in other people's ships and sucking stuff out?"

The three aliens huddled and whispered together. Astra heard the leader say "But the Horror told us there weren't any live ones in there" before he remembered to switch off his translator. She didn't really understand what he meant, and after the translator was switched off, she couldn't understand anything at all, of course. The aliens flapped their arms and eyestalks and floobed and plooged like three blocked gutters gurgling.

Then the leader turned his translator back on and said, "Come with us. We will take you to the captain."

They hauled her aboard their space scooter and set off through the bag, up the nozzle, and through an open air lock into the alien ship.

It was nothing like Astra's ship. It was a rusty, musty, dusty place, full of big plastic bins where the things that had been sucked from other ships were stored. Things that might have been cobwebs billowed from the battered ducting. Things that might have been candy wrappers drifted to and fro. It looked as if these aliens had never even heard of tidying up.

"Here we go!" the alien leader said, steering the scooter into an open area under a big

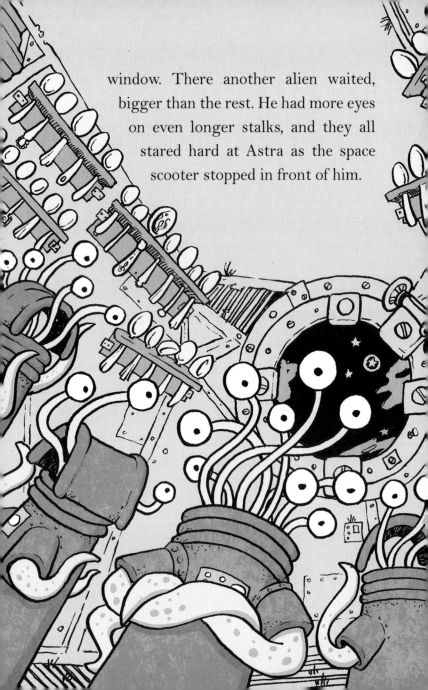

window. There another alien waited, bigger than the rest. He had more eyes on even longer stalks, and they all stared hard at Astra as the space scooter stopped in front of him.

The aliens took off their helmets and shook their eyestalks. Then plopped down onto the deck. Astra did the same. A green light had come on inside her helmet to show her that the air was safe to breathe. (Well, of course it was! Most of it had been stolen out of her ship!) But when she opened her visor and took a deep breath, it smelled strange and different, as if someone had been boiling vegetables in the alien ship for a long, long time.

The alien captain said some burbly, splurgy things to his crew, then activated his suit's translator and asked Astra, "Who are you? And what do you mean by cluttering up our collecting bag?"

Astra had had enough of this. Somehow, now that she'd seen how messy their ship was, she wasn't so frightened of these creatures. In place of fear she was starting to feel anger. "What do *you* mean," she shouted, "by stealing bits of my ship and cutting holes in it and vacuuming stuff out?"

The alien captain drew himself up to his full height and waved his eyestalks at her impressively. "Stealing?" he said. "We are not thieves. This is a salvage ship. We are the Poglites of Quarl, the best deep-space salvage experts this side of the Quinqagwah Scrap Moons. When we spy a drifting ship, we send our scouts aboard to make sure it's abandoned, then attach our collecting bag and suck out a sample of the salvage. And if it seems like good stuff, then we go aboard and begin dismantling it. The samples we have taken from this ship look promising, very promising. And then we find you. Who are you? Where did you come from? Do you work for the Quinqagwah Salvage

Corporation? Because if so, you can go straight back to your Scrap Moons and tell your masters that the Poglites of Quarl found this wreck first!"

"But it's not a wreck!" shouted Astra. "There are people on board! My mom and dad and baby brother, and loads of others!"

"She's lying!" said one of the other Poglites.

"That's not what our scout told us," said the captain.

"Then *he's* the one who's lying!" Astra said.

"The Nameless Horror does not lie," said the captain. "Aha! Here he is now. You can ask him yourself."

Astra looked behind her and gave a yelp of fear. Through the clutter maze of the Poglite ship, billowing like ink in water, came whispering and wafting the black tentacly oil-slick thing she'd met in Hibernation Section B.

"We call him the Nameless Horror," said the Poglite who'd first spoken to her, "because he's a horror, and he doesn't have a name. We found him adrift in empty space, in sector X19. He's very useful. He can change his

shape and sneak aboard ships to scout them out. He's the secret of our success."

"Be quiet, Poglite Two!" the captain snapped. "We do not need to share our secrets with this two-eyed snooper!"

The Nameless Horror, meanwhile, had settled on the deck in front of him and gathered itself into a sort of blob, which glistened faintly with reflections of the ship's dim lights. It wobbled horribly, like black jelly.

"Now then, Horror," said the Poglite captain. "Does this creature here look like she came off that ship we're salvaging? Or is she a spy from Quinqagwah?"

The Nameless Horror did not have any eyes, but Astra felt it looking at her. "Two eyes, two arms, two legs," it said. Its voice crackled through the Poglites' translators. "Yes. She is the same as the ones aboard that ship."

"But you told us there was no one aboard!"

"I said that there is no one *alive*," the Nameless Horror said. "That was before I saw this one. That ship is a tomb. I drifted all through it. It carries the bodies of the dead in glass coffins."

"There," said the captain. "No one alive. And dead bodies won't mind if we salvage their spoons and stuff, will they?"

"They aren't dead!" said Astra. "They're asleep!"

"Asleep?" the captain said.

"Asleep?" said the Nameless Horror. "I had not thought of that. Yes, perhaps she is right. Perhaps they are just sleeping."

"What, *all* of them?" asked the captain, waving his arms and eyestalks about angrily.

"We are on our way to Nova Mundi," said Astra. "It was going to be such a long journey that the ship put everyone to sleep until we got there."

"But you will never get there," said the Nameless Horror, and she could not tell if it was sadness or gloating that made its voice go so low and bubbling. "The ship's systems are failing. It is drifting off its course. It will not reach the sun that it was aimed at. It will miss it by a thousand million miles and go sailing on forever."

"Oh no!" said Astra in a little voice.

115

"Oh no!" said the Poglite captain in a big, firm one. "Oh no, it won't! Because we're going to go aboard and dismantle it to bits! Everyone asleep? What sort of stupid way is that to travel? They deserve to have their ship dismantled. And since they're all doomed anyway, I can't see what harm it does. Come on, mateys! We'll leave our robots to sort through the collecting bag. Let's go aboard and see what spoons and treasures these dozy sleepers have brought for us!"

The Poglites cheered and, clumping to cupboards and lockers in the ship's walls, began fetching out all kinds of tools.

"You can't!" wailed Astra. "You mustn't! You said you were salvage experts, but if you pull our ship to bits, it will be pirating and stealing and murder!"

A few of the Poglites stopped what they were doing to look thoughtfully at her, but the captain just thumped them and shoved them on their way.

"It's dangerous!" Astra warned.

That got their attention, all right. Even the captain stopped and stared at her.

"That's why the ship has gone off course," she explained. "That's why everything is going wrong! There are dangerous cakes on board!"

The Poglites' eyestalks waved like fronds of seaweed when the tide turns. A few of them looked down at the translator knobs on their spacesuits, and some tapped them as if they were broken.

The captain said, "I'm sorry? I thought you said 'dangerous cakes.'"

"That's what I did say!" Astra sketched big cake shapes in the air to show them exactly what they were dealing with. "Killer cupcakes! Ferocious fudge! Deadly doughnuts! They'll eat you alive!"

For a second more, the Poglite crew stood staring. Then the captain turned blue and started to make a strange "Kuk-kuk-kuk-kuk-kuk!" noise, and all the others followed suit, bouncing up and down. That was how Poglites laughed, Astra realized. They were all laughing at her.

"Come on," said the captain. "We've listened to enough of the alien's lies. People eat cakes, not the other way around."

"Are you sure, Captain?" asked one of the Poglites who'd picked Astra out of the collecting bag.

"Of course I'm sure, Ploodle! It's nature's way, whatever world you come from. But if the little alien knows what cakes are, there are bound to be spoons aplenty aboard that ship."

"HURRAH!" the Poglites cheered, and began rummaging even more furiously in their lockers, pulling out backpacks and collecting jars, electric saws and headlamps, pliers and lock picks and wrenches and all sorts of tools that Astra didn't recognize, but that she guessed were just what you needed if you were planning to take a spaceship apart and steal everything it carried.

"And what about the little alien, Captain?" asked the Poglite who'd been worried about the cakes.

"Take her spacesuit, Ploodle," the captain ordered. "Then chuck her away. Out of the air lock with her. That's what we do with useless space junk."

"But, Captain . . . ," the Nameless Horror said. Its smooth surface broke into writhing tentacles. Astra was afraid that it was going to tell the captain not to throw her out because it wanted to eat her.

But the captain was busy strapping on a huge mechanized set of salvage grabbers, and he wasn't interested in listening to the Name-less Horror. "You keep out of this, Horror," he said. "Get in your jar, and stay there until we come back."

The Nameless Horror reared up into a tall black column, and for a moment it towered over the captain as if it was going to eat *him*, not Astra. Then it seemed to melt, subsiding

back into an oil slick. On the far side of the ship stood a big, clear plastic jar, and the Horror rippled its way across the deck and poured itself inside, filling it up like ink.

"Well, get to work, Ploodle," the captain ordered.

Ploodle stood staring at Astra, blushing faintly mauve. "B-but what if she bites me or something?" she asked.

"You read too many space adventures, Ploodle," snapped the captain. "I'll leave Poglite Two here to help you. The rest of you, get a move on! Let me at them lovely spoons!"

And the Poglite crew followed him away through the ship toward the air lock, singing as they went. Their singing sounded like a whole bog full of frogs having a burping competition, but a few of them had accidentally left their translators switched on, so above the burps and belches Astra could make out what they were singing:

Through darkest night
And strange stars' light
And pale forgotten moons

Across the sky
We Poglites fly
In search of Lovely Spoons

Oh SPOONS SPOONS
SPOONY SPOONY SPOONS
SPOONY SPOONY SPOONY
SPOONY SPOONS

But one by one the forgetful Poglites remembered, or were thumped by the captain and told to switch off their translators, and by the time they reached the air lock and filed out through the collecting bag toward Astra's ship, all she could hear was:

Burp Burp Burp
Burp BUUURRP
Burp BURP Burp
BUUURRP
Burp-a burpy BURPP

SEVEN

Poglite Two and Ploodle stood looking at Astra.

"Well, let's get on with it," grumbled Poglite Two. "Otherwise there'll be no spoons left for us."

"What is it with you lot and spoons?" asked Astra.

"Spoons are the most valuable thing on Quarl!" said Poglite Two, looking shocked that anyone could be so ignorant. "We Poglites are a wise and ancient civilization, but we have never managed to develop spoon technology, so we rely on the spoons we can gather from other races. That's why we seven ventured on this long voyage. We shall return home as rich Poglites, our pockets bulging with spoons!"

He grabbed the collar of Astra's spacesuit and started to detach her helmet. But as the helmet came off, Mammoth, who had been nestled all this time against Astra's chest, popped out through the suit's wide neck hole and wobbled up into the air.

The eyestalks of the two Poglites craned to follow him. Their wide eyes grew still wider, and they turned purple with excitement.

"Look!" said Poglite Two.

"It is Broknar himself!" said Ploodle.

And before Astra knew what they were

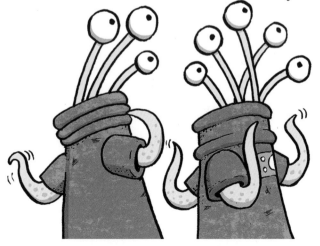

doing, they had knelt down before the floating Mammoth. It wasn't easy for them to kneel in zero gravity, but they managed it, and there they knelt, their round bottoms poking up into the air, their many eyeballs swiveling to follow the wavery course that Mammoth took across the room, until Astra went after him and caught him.

"He's only a cuddly toy," Astra said, feeling a little bit embarrassed, in case the aliens thought she was too old for cuddlies. "He's made of fur and stuffing and stuff. Look."

She held Mammoth out and squeezed him so that the Poglites could see he was just a toy. They clambered to their feet again.

"So even these two-armed, two-eyed

aliens have heard of Broknar the Sky Beast!" said Ploodle. She went over to a hatch in the wall—an overdecorated hatch, covered in swirly patterns, precious stones, and shining star shapes made from old spoons—and opened it to reveal a shrine to Broknar. He had more eyes and legs than Mammoth, but he had a trunk and two long, twirling tusks, so it was easy to see how the Poglites had confused them.

"Do all your people carry the image of Broknar with them?" asked Poglite Two.

"No," said Astra. "Just me."

"Ah! Then that explains why Broknar saved you and left all the others to sleep on while we stole their spoons!" said Ploodle.

"*Salvaged* their spoons, Ploodle, not stole."

"Sorry, Poglite Two. But if Broknar chose to save her, he will be angry if we throw her out of the air lock! Great will be his wrathful

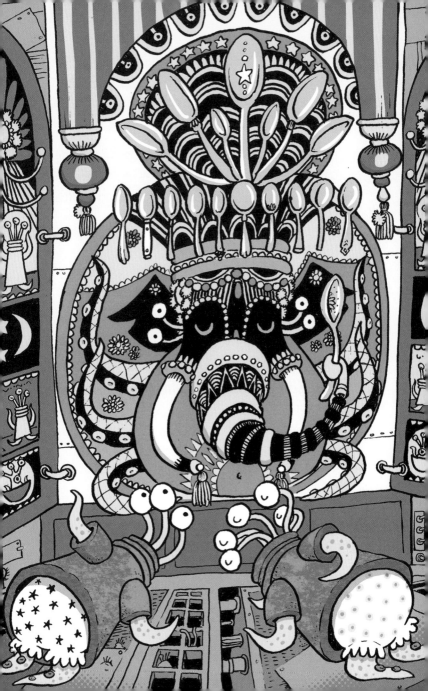

trumpetings, and his mighty tentacles will stomp our spoon collections!"

Both Poglites flushed purple with fear.

"What shall we do?" asked Poglite Two.

"We must not harm her. Let's leave her here. The captain can decide what to do with her."

"Good idea."

They bundled Astra into one of the empty lockers and shut the door. After a moment Ploodle opened the door and handed her a plastic globe filled with something purple. "A nice, nourishing ball of gloop," she said, "in case you get hungry." Then she closed the door again.

* * *

Astra sat in the shadows. She looked at the globe Ploodle had given her. The stuff inside it slopped about stickily, looking as if some-

one had mashed up a load of fat purple worms, and not even done it very well, because some of them still seemed to be wriggling. She supposed that this must be a Poglite's idea of a tasty snack. She hoped she wouldn't ever get hungry enough to feel like eating it. But she put it into the pocket in the front of her spacesuit, just in case.

She heard the clumping footfalls as

Ploodle and Poglite Two went stomping off to join their friends, who were probably pulling her ship to pieces by now. She tried the door, but it was locked. She looked around the inside of the locker for something that might help her escape. A few bits and pieces were stuffed in between narrow shelves at the back or floated around her, tethered to hooks on the walls. But bits and pieces of what? They could have been machinery or works of art or sleeping pets for all she knew.

Then, just as she was admitting to herself that she was stuck there until the Poglites returned, there was a click, and the door opened.

At first, Astra thought that it had opened of its own accord. She peeked out, but the hold of the Poglite ship was still and silent. Then she noticed something like a long strand of black spaghetti laid across the floor in front of her. It led back to the plastic jar where the Nameless Horror lived.

So that was who had opened the door!

The spaghetti tentacle withdrew, and the Nameless Horror came glooping out of its vat. It oozed across the deck toward her. *Oh no!* thought Astra. *Now that the Poglites have cleared off, it's definitely going to eat me!*

She braced herself against the locker wall and then sprang out, as far and as fast as she could. Through the air above the Horror's groping tentacles she flew, graceful as an acrobat. Her helmet, which Ploodle and Poglite Two had taken off, bobbed against the grubby ceiling like a lost balloon after a party. She grabbed it, kicked off from a fat bit of duct, and went hurtling back the other way.

The Nameless Horror groped and snatched at her with long black tentacles like licorice bootlaces. She avoided all of them and flew/swam/flung herself through the mucky ship toward the open air lock. Behind her, the gloopy, bubbling voice of the Horror rose.

She thought it was trying to form words, but there were no handy Poglites standing about with their translating machines switched on, so she could not understand it.

Fastening her helmet as she went, she dived at the air lock. She didn't really need the helmet, of course, because the Poglites' collecting bag was still attached, forming a tunnel of air between the two ships.

Poglite robots were busy there, herding the drifting clutter into bundles and tying the bundles together with brown hairy string. They didn't notice Astra as she went blundering through the bag. They didn't even notice when she kicked off from one of their

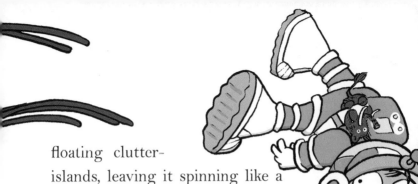

floating clutter-islands, leaving it spinning like a scruffy merry-go-round.

In the Poglite ship, the Nameless Horror fumbled a locker open and pulled out an empty Poglite spacesuit. It stuck a bit of itself inside and switched on the translator with a tentacle.

"Astra!" it said. "Come back!"

But by that time Astra was already groping her way back through her own ship's air lock, into the shadows of the cake-haunted, Poglite-ridden corridors.

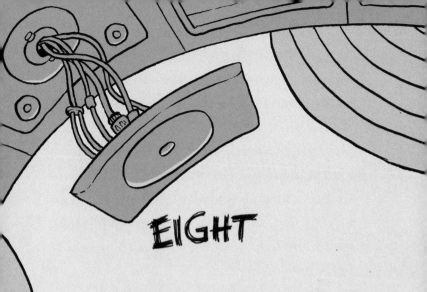

EIGHT

At first, Astra saw no sign of Poglites or cakes. Everything was quiet. Nothing moved except a few bits of fluff, tumbling about in the air currents.

"Pilbeam!" Astra called softly.

There was no reply. Maybe the little robot had set off for the control room alone. Maybe he was already there, sorting out the cake problem and setting the ship to rights.

Or maybe he had been sucked out after her and was buried in one of those clutter-clumps outside. In which case it was up to *her* to go to the control room. . . .

But first, as everything seemed so quiet, she decided that she would nip back to Hibernation Section C and make sure that her family was sleeping soundly. She was still half hoping that they might have woken up. How could anybody have slept through all those cakes and sirens?

No cakes leapt at her as she made her way back along the passages, stopping now and then to check the big color-coded maps that were mounted on the walls at intersections. Once she turned a corner and found a cupcake hanging in the air ahead of her, but it scooted off fearfully when it saw her coming, leaving a faint smell of marzipan behind it. She passed a few floating crumbs as well, but otherwise there was no sign of cakes.

No sign of Poglites, either, except when some far-off footsteps and a gleeful shout of "Spoons!" came echoing down a side passage.

When she reached Hibernation Section C, she looked for a long time through the glass porthole in the door, but nothing moved in there, so she went inside. The door that led to the dining hall was shut again. She put her ear against it and heard the faint whizz and whir of Nom-O-Tron. She floated over to the pods where Mom and Dad and Alf were sleeping. She looked in at them. How she wished that she could wake them! Tears came out of her eyes and wobbled off, drifting away through the hall of silent sleepers like tiny, shimmering balloons.

"Please return to your pod!" said an abrupt, robotic voice behind her.

"Eek!" squeaked Astra, turning. It was difficult for her to stop moving once she'd started, so she kept revolving, spinning there in midair above her family's sleeping faces.

"Stop rotating and return to your pod!" ordered Bedbot. "Passengers must remain asleep for the duration of the voyage. Return to your pod and prepare for re-sedation."

"No," said Astra. "I can't!"

"The emergency alarm in this compartment was activated," said Bedbot. "I am here to re-sedate you. Return to your pod."

"That was hours ago!" Astra complained.

"Five hours, thirty-one minutes, and seven seconds," said Bedbot fussily. "No other Bedbot was available to respond to your request. I have come all the way from Hibernation Section F. I was unable to reach you sooner."

"Poor Bedbot!" said Astra. "But you don't understand, I need to stay awake. There are these cakes, and these Poglites. . . ."

"My data banks do not recognize the word 'Poglites,'" said Bedbot. "Return to your pod."

The lid of Astra's pod opened. It looked snuggly and inviting in there. But if she climbed in and went to sleep, who would save the ship?

Bedbot reached out an extendable metal arm and grabbed her by one ankle, trying to drag her toward the pod. She wriggled free.

"Listen," she said. "When I pressed that button, I *did* want to go back in my pod. But things have changed now. My pod woke me because something's gone wrong with the ship. We're infested with dangerous cakes! I have to go to the control room and restart the computer so that the ship can get rid of them!"

But Bedbot didn't care about any of that. She hadn't been programmed to think about aliens. "Return to your pod," she said. "If you do not return to your pod, you will be forcibly re-sedated." She extended another arm, and in this one was a syringe full of a bright liquid.

Astra stared at it. "What's that?"

"A harmless sleeping drug. Passengers who refuse to comply with my requests must

be forcibly sedated," said the robot. She made a lunge with the syringe. Astra grabbed her arm, and instead of squirting the fluid into her leg, the syringe shot it harmlessly past her, a constellation of droplets tumbling away to join her drifting tears.

"I can't go to sleep!" shouted Astra. "If I'm asleep, I'll be helpless, like everybody else! I have to save the ship!"

Bedbot just said again that passengers who refused to comply would be forcibly sedated. Anchoring herself firmly to the floor with magnets, Bedbot loaded the syringe with another dose. "Do not be alarmed," she said. "Sleep is good for you. Your dreams will be pleasant. When you awake, we will be at our destination."

"But we won't!" yelled Astra. "We're far off course! The ship . . . ! The Poglites . . . ! The cakes . . . !"

Bedbot reached out another arm and

grabbed Astra by the neck of her suit. Bedbot meant to hold her still this time while she injected her.

"Bedtime!" she said in a chirpy, syrupy voice. "Sweet dreams!"

Astra unzipped the pocket on the front of her spacesuit. She pulled out the disgusting-looking packed lunch that Ploodle had given her. She took off the lid and flung the whole lot at Bedbot.

Squerch. The sticky, writhing mess landed smack in the middle of the robot's face and stuck there, plastered across her sensor eye. Bedbot stopped trying to inject Astra and said, "I cannot see! Please remove the obstruction!"

"Let me go!" said Astra, kicking and wriggling, trying to pry the robot's metal hand off her suit collar.

Bedbot put the syringe away and started trying to wipe the sticky mess off her eye.

Astra unzipped her spacesuit. She kicked and wriggled her way out of it, stuffing Mammoth quickly into her waistband yet again.

I'm getting pretty good at escaping, she thought, kicking Bedbot as hard as she could with both feet and somersaulting away from her toward the door.

But the door had closed behind her as she came in, and to open it again she would have to stop and operate the door controls. Behind her she could hear the stomping magnetic footfalls of Bedbot as she wiped the gloop from her face and started after Astra. Would there be time?

The door opened, startling her. The eddying air carried her through it, and there in the corridor outside she found Pilbeam waiting.

"Pilbeam!"

"Greetings, Astra," said the robot. He closed the door again, muffling Bedbot's angry shouts.

"Oh, Pilbeam!" she said, hugging him. "Did you get to the control room? Have you put the ship right?"

Pilbeam shook his head. "I'm sorry, Astra. Those cakes must have found another way out of the dining hall. They are all over the ship! They attack anything that moves! I was ambushed by a Swiss roll on the way to the control room, and I had to turn back."

"That's funny," said Astra. "I didn't see any just now. I came all the way back from the air lock, and there wasn't a big cake to be seen. Only a few crumbs."

"They must have found something else to hunt," said Pilbeam, giving a little mechanical shudder as he remembered his own narrow escape.

Astra gasped. "The Poglites!"

"The who?"

"It doesn't matter. Come on, let's get to the control room while the cakes are busy eating them. If there was ever anybody who deserved to be eaten by a cake, it's those Poglites!"

They drifted on along the corridors, but after a little way Astra started to feel guilty about what she had said, and after a little while more, she stopped.

"No, they don't," she told Pilbeam. "They aren't all bad: Ploodle and Poglite Two were quite kind, really, giving me that gloop and everything. I think the captain is the only really bad one, and even he doesn't deserve to be caked. We have to warn them."

Pilbeam's head went around once or twice in a thoughtful way. "Come on!" he said.

Taking Astra by the hand, he drew her down a side passage to a small room whose walls were covered with all kinds of screens. Big screens, little screens, round screens, square screens, oblong screens . . . If you liked screens, thought Astra, this was the place for you.

"What is this place?" she asked.

"I keep watch on the ship from here," said

Pilbeam. "When I'm not zooming around mending bits of it, which is most of the time."

He touched some switches, and the screens filled with video views of the sleeping ship. Empty corridors, silently glowing sleep pods, even views across the spooky metal moonscapes of the outer hull, and the Poglite ship attached by its collecting-bag tunnel. Everything seemed still. They might as well have been photographs, thought Astra, looking from one to the next. Then she saw a dark shape go past a camera on one of the lower decks.

"What was that?" She leaned closer, then jumped back as a ferocious fruitcake peered right into the camera, raisins glistening.

"Eek!" she said. "I never knew cakes could be so scary! And it had whole cherries stuck in it. I hate those!"

"Astra! Astra, look!" said Pilbeam. "It's Sub-Corridor G2!"

On the screen he was pointing
to, the plump, dumpy figures of the Poglites
were stumping along a corridor, using their
arms to grip the walls and deck. They must
have been looting the supply cupboards down
in that part of the ship, because Astra could
see spoons glinting in their bags and pockets,
and a few carried larger bits of salvage. There
were seven of them. "So Ploodle and Poglite
Two caught up with their friends," she said.
"I wonder if they've found out about the cakes
yet."

"I think they're about to," said Pilbeam
nervously. "Look what's waiting for them in
Sub-Corridor G3!"

Astra looked at the next screen. At first,
all she could see were the ducts and pipes and
striped candy-cane tubes that covered the
sides of Sub-Corridor G3. Then, in the shadows between them, she saw movement.

Lots of movement.

A bristling of sprinkles.

A quivering of confectioner's custard.

"Pilbeam," she squeaked, "some of those cakes have *arms and legs!*"

"Yes, Astra."

"*Lots* of arms and legs!"

"They have been evolving very fast."

"We have to warn the Poglites!"

There was a sound button next to the screen with the Poglites on it. Astra poked it, and their voices filled the little room, tinny and burbly and completely impossible to understand, except for Ploodle, who had forgotten to turn off her translator and was saying, "You'll never guess what I found in that last cupboard: sporks! They're like spoons, but they have a forky part, too!"

Poglite Two hadn't turned off his translator, either. "Oh, Ploodle," he said, "everyone knows a spork isn't nearly as valuable as a spoon."

"Poglites!" Astra shouted, and they all bumped into one another and dropped their spoons and salvage tools as they looked about in alarm to see where her voice had come from.

They shouted, "Ploogah stoofi!" and "Weebo!"

The captain switched his translator on and yelled, "Who said that?"

"It's me!" Astra shouted. "I'm watching you on-screen, and there are cakes lurking just around the corner! Run away! Quickly!"

"So you've escaped, have you?" growled the Poglite captain. "You still think you can scare us with your cakes? We are Poglites! We eat cakes for breakfast! Well, not really for breakfast—that would be weird—but we eat them for afternoon tea. . . ."

He looked behind him. His crew was a little more worried about Astra's warning than he was. He waved them forward with his salvage grabbers. "Come on, Poglites. More spoons to be had down here!"

"I can't watch!" wailed Astra, and she put her hands over her eyes so she wouldn't have to.

But that didn't stop her from hearing what happened next. The yell of surprise from the Poglite captain as he turned the corner. The roar of the cakes as they sprang from their hiding places. The confused crashing and banging and splatting and shouting, mostly in Poglite, but through it all the translated voice of Ploodle yelling, "Astra! Help!"

A less kindhearted girl than Astra would just have said, "I told you so." A part of her did say that. Whatever horrible cakey things

were happening to those Poglites, it wasn't anybody's fault but their own. And yet . . . She opened her fingers just a crack and saw a great tumble of movement on the screen. Then a tumbling cake splattered against the camera and the screen went black.

"Pilbeam," she said, "we have to help them!"

"But, Astra . . ."

She was already throwing herself through the door. Pilbeam shrugged and followed her.

Out in the corridor again, Astra could dimly hear the sounds of the cake-versus-Poglite scuffle going on a few decks below. (Or was it above? It was so hard to remember which was which, without any gravity to set you straight.) She pulled herself along by the handholds in the walls until she was flying at a fair speed toward the source of the noises. Pilbeam came whizzing along behind her, and soon caught up. "This way," he said. "Now down here—but please be careful."

They sped through a long tube, and suddenly they were at the scene of the battle.

It was completely quiet.

It was completely deserted.

The air was full of drifting crumbs, and there were great splashes of icing and custard on the walls. Dropped Poglite tools and weapons tumbled about in midair. There were a lot of spoons. A bag came bobbing toward Astra and she grabbed it and looked inside. Strange forky little spoon-things glinted in there, like fish. "Sporks," she said. "This was Ploodle's bag. Oh, Ploodle!" She looped the bag's strap over her head. She felt frightened and a little bit teary, but mostly now she felt cross. All this bother, just because stupid old Nom-O-Tron hadn't turned itself off.

"That's it!" she shouted. "I have had it with these dumb cakes on this dumb spaceship!"

"Astra," said Pilbeam suddenly. "Behind you!"

She spun around, expecting a menacing muffin or a wicked whoopie pie.

Instead, she saw the Nameless Horror.

NINE

It stretched from floor to ceiling like a shiny black curtain, billowing slightly in the gentle breeze that blew along the passageway. It bulged and heaved and reached out a dozen oily tentacles that came snaking and twining toward Astra. Some of them wrapped around Pilbeam like the tentacles of some evil plant.

"Astra, run!" shouted Pilbeam.

Astra started to back away, but when she looked behind her, she saw more trouble there. A cake was blocking the corridor.

A really big cake.

It looked a little like a mutant cinnamon roll, but with teeth. Also, thought Astra, cinnamon rolls didn't have all those legs and claws. And they didn't growl like that.

The cake sprang at her. At the same moment, one of the Horror's tentacles wrapped around her from behind. The killer cake hissed in fury as Astra was jerked away from it.

The Nameless Horror moved fast, growing legs when it needed them to gallop along the walls and floor and ceiling of the passageways, sometimes turning almost entirely liquid and just pouring. Gripped tightly in its tentacles, Astra and Pilbeam went rushing through the ship nearly as fast as Astra had when the Poglites vacuumed her up.

When the rushing stopped, they were back in the garden where Astra had eaten the peach.

Now she knew how the peach might have felt when she plucked it from its nice, comfortable branch and bared her teeth to bite into it. The Nameless Horror let go of her and she drifted beside Pilbeam above the overgrown lawn, waiting nervously for it to eat her.

Instead, the Horror began to change. It drew in its inky tentacles and seemed to shrink, gathering itself into a glistening blob of black ooze as tall as a man. A head bulged like a bud on top of it. Features appeared there as if an invisible sculptor was molding a face out of wet black clay. The blob stretched out one arm and then another. The arms grew hands, and the hands grew fingers, which wiggled experimentally. Its lower half divided into legs, with broad, flat, five-toed feet that stuck somehow to the lawn despite the lack of gravity. It was ten feet tall, a giant of shining darkness. With careful steps it walked toward Astra.

"I do not want to eat you," it said.

"You speak English!"

"I studied the Poglites' translator logs and learned your language."

"Oh . . ."

"Perhaps I will not frighten you so much now that I look more like a human."

Astra watched the black giant come toward her. He did not look *much* like a human, and he was still a little frightening. But he seemed quite polite, so she said, "I'm Astra. What's your name?"

"I am the Nameless Horror."

"But that's not a name!" said Astra. "That's just what those Poglites call you. What's your real name? What does your family call you?"

"I am the Nameless Horror," the Nameless Horror said. "That is the only thing I have ever been called. I do not have any family, except the Poglites."

Astra frowned, remembering what Poglite Two had said about the Nameless Horror. "They found you drifting in space," she said. "Were you on another ship they robbed?"

"I was not on a ship," said the Nameless Horror. "I was just drifting. And then along came the Poglite ship and took me in. And when they found that I could alter my shape and live in the emptiness of space and slither easily inside other ships, they thought I could be useful to them and let me stay."

Perhaps he *was* the emptiness of space, thought Astra. Perhaps a bit of all that emptiness got tired of being nothing and turned itself somehow into him. And then it didn't know what to do and just floated there, waiting, until the Poglites arrived and told it what to be.

"Thank you for letting me out," she said.

The Nameless Horror said, "It is wrong, what they are doing to your ship. They told me that they only took things that no one needed anymore. It is my fault. I thought your people were all dead. I thought this was a great tomb, in which some alien race had sent the bodies of their beloved dead to fly among the far stars forever. By the time the Poglites learned of my mistake, their greed had got the better of them."

"It's not your fault," said Astra. "It's mine. That's what caused it all. Those cakes . . . That's what made the ship go off course. And now the Poglites have been eaten, even the nice ones, and it's my fault, all of it. . . ." She clenched her fists tight to stop herself from crying again.

"They have not been eaten," said the Nameless Horror. "I can feel them faintly. I can hear their voices, vibrating through the walls of the ship. They are prisoners."

"Why would cakes want prisoners?" asked Pilbeam.

"These are no ordinary cakes," said Astra. "Who knows what they want? Poor Poglites! I suppose we shall have to rescue them."

"No," said Pilbeam. "It is more important that we get to the control room and try to regain control of the ship."

The Nameless Horror had been watching them. He was picking up some of their gestures and expressions to go with his new body. He nodded, and then let his head revolve like Pilbeam's.

"If we go together," he said, "we can do both."

TEN

They went back to the room of screens, but there was no sign of the cakes on any of them.

"Where are they?" asked Astra. "I thought you said we could see the whole ship from here."

Pilbeam pointed to a small screen that fizzed with gray snow. "Look! That's the camera in the dining hall. The cakes must have switched it off so we couldn't see them!"

"Would they know how to do that?" asked Astra.

"They have been getting more and more intelligent."

169

Astra looked at the Nameless Horror, wondering how much of this he understood. Poor Horror—he had probably never even seen an ordinary cake, let alone a ferocious man-eating one.

"I asked Nom-O-Tron 9000 to make me the ultimate cake," she said. "That's how all this started. It's been churning out cakes ever since, and they've been evolving and learning and fighting each other. I suppose it makes sense that they would think of the dining hall as home. . . ."

"Then that is where they will have taken the Poglites," said the Nameless Horror. "And that is where we will go."

Pilbeam unscrewed the ventilation grille on an air shaft. They all scrambled inside, and Pilbeam led them through the tight twists and turns of the shaft until they reached another grille.

Cakey, marzipany smells came in through

the grille. Strange grunting sounds and muf-
fled whimperings. Astra edged over and put
her face to it. She was looking into the dining
hall. There was the great blind face of Nom-
O-Tron, and the savage cakes. Each of them
carried what looked at first like a big traffic
cone. Then Astra realized that the traffic-cone
things were the Poglites; they had pulled in
their hands and feet and eyestalks and tugged
down the lids of their chimney-pot spacesuits
so that the cakes could not get at them. Perhaps they had hoped that the cakes would
give up trying and lose interest in them.

But the cakes had other plans. Smeared on
the walls and floor of the hall were big splats
of icing, left over from fearsome cake-versus-
cake battles that must have happened while
Astra was aboard the Poglite ship. The cakes
now scooped up the sticky stuff and started
to splodge it over the whimpering Poglites,
encasing them in icing. Some had got icing

bags from somewhere, and set about decorating the iced Poglites with pretty curlicues and squirls of piping in pastel pink and baby blue. Others went around gathering the sprinkles and candy flowers that floated in the hall and added them to the Poglites, too.

"What are they doing?" asked the Nameless Horror, squeezing up next to Astra to have a look.

"They're icing them!" said Astra. "They're trying to make them look prettier, I think. I suppose to a cake, the more icing you have, the prettier you are. . . ."

"Is icing dangerous?" asked the Horror.

"My mom says it's bad for your teeth," said Astra. "But it's not like the Poglites are eating it. . . . I suppose they might suffocate in there, though."

The cakes had finished their work. They pushed the iced mass of Poglites toward Nom-O-Tron. A fearsome-looking cupcake, larger than the rest, raised its arms and said in a crumbly voice, "O Great Cake Maker! Accept these sacrifices! Make us more cake warriors to do your bidding!"

"*Now* what?" whispered Astra. She was a little bit surprised that the cakes had learned

to talk, but what worried her more was the long nozzle that came whirring out of the front of Nom-O-Tron like an elephant's trunk.

"They are feeding your friends to the machine!" said Pilbeam. "That's the nozzle it uses to suck up bits of uneaten food so it can be recycled."

"But Poglites aren't table scraps!" hissed Astra. "What will happen to them?"

"They'll be turned into cakes," said Pilbeam.

"That's awful!"

"Yes, I should think they'll taste horrid. . . ."

"We have to stop them!" said the Nameless Horror.

"How?" said Astra. "We need to think! We can't just go bursting into the dining hall. . . ."

But there was no time to think. Scrunched

together like that, the three of them had put too much pressure on the ventilator grille. *Schlink*, it went as it gave way, and they tumbled out into the dining hall in a higgledy-piggledy heap.

The cakes turned, surprised to see this bundle of legs and arms and tentacles somersaulting toward them. Then, leaving the captive Poglites drifting helplessly, they sprang to the attack.

"Stay back!" warned Astra. She pulled a spork from her bag and brandished it like a dagger. "We have sporks, and we're not afraid to use them!"

The cakes wavered a little. A lot of them were from an earlier batch, and not quite as bright as their leader. They were bright enough to fear the spork, though; it looked to them like a cake fork, the traditional enemy of all cakes.

But the king cake just laughed and waved the others on. "Does she think she can frighten us with her puny spork? There was a time when humans ate us, but that time is over! This is the age of the cake! Attack!"

Astra upended the bag, scattering a tumble of sporks. Pilbeam snatched two, and the Nameless Horror took the rest, stretching himself big and thin until he formed a sort of wall between Astra and Pilbeam and the onrushing cakes, a wall waving with tentacles, and in every tentacle a bright spork.

"I'll hold them off, Astra!" the Nameless Horror shouted. "You talk to Nom-O-Tron!"

"But what good will that do?"

"You said it started this. It can make it stop!"

The cakes thudded into the Nameless Horror and rebounded as if he was a trampoline. Astra grabbed Pilbeam's hand and let the little robot fly her across the hall to Nom-O-Tron. The nozzle on the front of the machine was busily trying to suck up the iced Poglite captain, but he had wedged halfway. Bits of his icing had broken off, and one

179

of his eyestalks poked out and focused franti-
cally on Astra.

"Help!" he shouted.

Astra looked over her shoulder, to where the Nameless Horror was holding his ground amid a flurry of cakes and sporks.

Well-aimed spork blows sliced great chunks out of the furious cakes, and the air was filled with a spreading cloud of crumbs, raisins, cake decorations, and candied cherries. But the cakes were fighting back. Big rips and tears were appearing in the blackness of the Nameless Horror. He was starting to

181

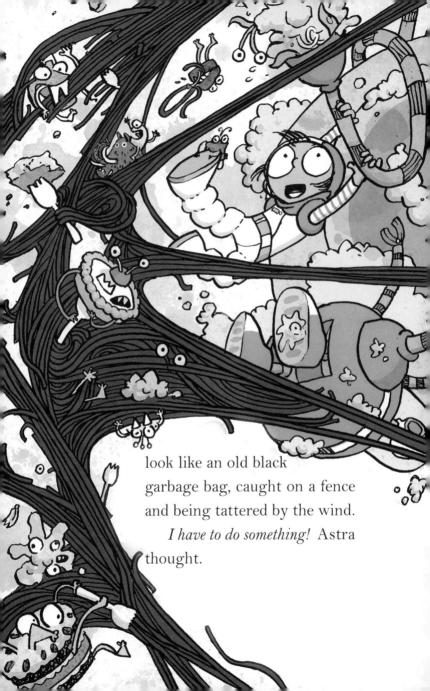

look like an old black
garbage bag, caught on a fence
and being tattered by the wind.

I have to do something! Astra
thought.

"Nom-O-Tron, stop!" she shouted, though she didn't think it would work.

She was right. Nom-O-Tron kept on trying to suck in the Poglite captain. "Nom-O-Tron is busy," it said. "Still attempting to comply with your previous request."

"What, when I asked for a cake?"

"You requested the ultimate cake," said Nom-O-Tron.

"But I didn't mean that!" wailed Astra. "Anyway, it was a hundred years ago! I don't even want cake anymore! I've gone right off cake! I don't think I'll ever want to eat a cake again!"

"I cannot accept further instructions until I have developed the most advanced cake possible," said Nom-O-Tron in its annoying way.

Astra glanced over her shoulder again. It was hard to tell, what with him being a Nameless Horror and everything, but she thought that the Nameless Horror was getting tired, while the angry cakes fought just as furiously as ever.

She decided to try talking to Nom-O-Tron one last time.

"*These* are your idea of advanced cakes?" she demanded, as scathingly as she could manage.

"They are superior cakes," said Nom-O-Tron. Was it just Astra's imagination, or did the food machine sound a little bit defensive? "They are stronger and more intelligent than all previous batches," it continued. "Capable of working together to defend themselves. Some of them have acidic fillings."

"Ow!" shouted the Nameless Horror as he sporked a plump cake and a jet of acid shot out and scorched another hole in him.

"Well, I think they *stink*!" said Astra.

"Define 'stink,'" said Nom-O-Tron. It sounded slightly hurt.

"I wanted a nice cake! I didn't want cakes

with claws and teeth and bad attitudes! And who on earth would want a cake that had acid for a filling? I think you need to vacuum all this up and try again."

Nom-O-Tron whirred and creaked for a moment. Then it snorted out the Poglite captain, who yelled "Aaieeee! Oh! Ouch!" as he went rebounding around the dining hall like a pinball. The elephant-trunk-nozzle-thing stretched out across the hall and—*glop! glop!*

glop! GLOP!—sucked up the ferocious cakes one by one. Then it snuffled up all the floating bits and crumbs. Finally it snorted up a few raggedy bits of the Nameless Horror that the cakes had torn off.

Then it retracted very quickly into the front of the machine, a hatch closed over it, and all was quiet again.

"Phew!" said Pilbeam.

"You did it, Astra!" said the Nameless Horror.

"No, I just bought us a little time," said Astra. On the front of Nom-O-Tron the red sign was still flashing, just as it had flashed for a hundred long years while she was asleep.

WORKING
WORKING

"It's making another batch of cakes," she said, "and with our luck, the new ones will be even worse. . . ."

Pilbeam was breaking the Poglites out of their icing prisons. Astra went to help him, and then saw the Nameless Horror and stopped. The poor Horror was pulling himself back into human shape, but he was full of holes and all raggedy around the edges where the cakes had torn him with their teeth and claws.

"Oh, Nameless!" she said, scooting over to him and hugging him tight. "Are you very badly injured?"

"I do not know," said the Nameless Horror. "I have never been injured before." (He had never been hugged before, either. He was not sure quite what to make of it.)

Astra held him tight and wondered what to do. Nom-O-Tron would be producing more cakes in a moment, and she didn't think the Nameless Horror was in any state to fight them.

"Astra?" It was Ploodle, tugging at her sleeve. "Come with us! We will get aboard our own ship and escape before more cakes appear! We do not like your Earth cakes at all."

Poglite Two bobbed up beside her. "I am captain now. We have had a discussion, and decided that the captain is not fit to command us. He has been relieved of his spoons. Come with us! You will be safe aboard our ship."

"But I can't!" said Astra. "What about my family? What about everybody else?"

The Poglites all looked at each other and flushed pale pink with pity.

And from above them, in the maze of snaky ducts and jungle-vine plumbing on the ceiling, came a fearsome, cakey growl. The king cake, the best and fiercest, had leapt out of the way when Nom-O-Tron's nozzle had sucked up the rest. He had hidden up there on the ceiling, and now he emerged, baring his fearsome teeth. Nor was he alone. Lots of smaller cakes that had been hiding in the corners of the hall, afraid of the larger ones, had found new courage, and came creeping out. Sinister Swiss rolls and killer carrot cakes, beastly brownies and awful apple turnovers.

Pilbeam pushed Astra out of the way as the king cake lashed at her with his claws. He missed but caught Pilbeam instead. "Bother!" said the little robot as his head came off and went pinging across the hall.

"Oh, heavens!" said Astra, gripping her spork and getting ready to defend herself. "Oh, help!"

And from the far end of the hall, where Nom-O-Tron stood, there came a single, terrifying *PING*.

Astra looked around. The hatch where the new cakes came out was still shut, but behind it something moved. Fingers of light poked out around its edges, fluttering. Astra, the Poglites, and the Nameless Horror stared. Even the cakes that had been advancing stopped and watched as the hatch slid open.

Out into the hall came the most enormous, most beautiful cake that any of them had ever seen. Nom-O-Tron had whizzed up bits of all the other cakes and bits of the stuff the Nameless Horror was made out of—whatever *that* was—and somehow turned it all into this.

It had no arms or legs, as if Nom-O-Tron had finally understood that cakes had no need for such things. But it had many layers, like a wedding cake, and all the layers rippled as it pushed itself through the air, like a huge and beautiful jellyfish. It pulsed with patterns of light, and the rest of it was so pale and transparent that it seemed to be made of light. And was it just Astra's imagination, or did a sort of wordless singing like angel voices accompany it as it came to float before her?

"It's the ultimate cake!" she gasped. "Oh, Nom-O-Tron, you did it! It's so light, and so perfect! And I bet it's really tasty. . . ."

But of course she didn't try to find out. It was impossible to even think of cutting a slice of a cake that beautiful.

Then the Ultimate Cake spoke, and Astra could tell at once that some of the gentleness of the Nameless Horror had been baked into it. It said, "What is this, my cakes? Fear and fighting?"

"What else is there?" said the king cake.

"Nothing, if you stay in this world of humans, who see us only as tasty snacks," the Ultimate Cake said. "So come with me, and we shall find some unknown world where we may begin anew, where cakes may live in harmony together. Come with me, to the Planet of the Cakes!"

"The Planet of the Cakes!" the king cake whispered. Some of the lesser cakes around him echoed the words, and even the older ones that didn't have the power of speech made crumby, woffly noises, trying to join in. "The Planet of the Cakes! The Planet of the Cakes!"

And then the great cake turned and went rippling and wafting from the hall, through the doors that opened obediently to let it out. And the other cakes all followed, and so did Astra, because she somehow knew that they would do her no harm now that the Ultimate Cake was there to protect her.

Along the ship's corridors they flew, one girl in a cloud of cakes, until they reached an air lock on the opposite side of the ship from the Poglite's bag. The inner door slid open without anybody touching the controls, as if the Ultimate Cake had simply brushed it with its mind. The cakes all bundled inside, jostling each other in their eagerness but not fighting anymore. Some were giggling with anticipation; others kept saying, "The Planet of the Cakes! We are going to the Planet of the Cakes!"

Astra almost followed them, she was so caught up in their cakey excitement. But the Ultimate Cake gently pushed her away. "No, Astra," it said kindly. "You must stay here, with your family and your friends."

Then it went after the others into the air lock, and the door closed behind it. Astra watched the lights on the control panel change from green to red to show that the outer door had opened. Then she ran along the corridor to a window and looked out.

Out of the ship the cloud of cakes went pouring: cupcakes and cake pops, red velvet and funnel cakes, sponge cakes and double chocolate fudge, and strange nameless cakes out of Nom-O-Tron's imaginings. And in the

midst of the cloud floated the great, glowing shape of the Ultimate Cake, shining so brightly that Astra could see it for a long time, long after all the littler ones had dwindled into the darkness and the silence of space.

* * *

"Well," Astra said to herself, "that was a little weird."

And she hurried back to her friends.

ELEVEN

The Poglites had already repaired Pilbeam when Astra returned to the dining hall. In another half hour, she and the Nameless Horror were sitting in the big, comfy swivel chairs in the control room, watching while the little robot repaired the ship's computer.

"Goodbye, Astra!" called the Poglites. "Goodbye, Nameless Horror!" Their ship circled Astra's three times as they checked that their robots had put back all the bits they'd started to remove. They had returned almost all the things they'd sucked out of it, too, although Astra had said they could keep most of the spoons. They would be so rich that they would never need to go spoon hunting again, so they did not mind too much that the Nameless Horror had decided not to go with them. "We'll make our fortunes with all this lovely spoonage," they chuckled. "And though your ship doesn't *look* quite as neat as before, it will all work. Goodbye! May Broknar protect you on your new world!"

"Goodbye!" said Astra, waving at their images on one of the control-room screens. She held Mammoth up and waved his trunk

at them. She felt sorry to see them go, and as their ship accelerated away and their signal faded, she went over to the Nameless Horror and hugged him. "When we get to Nova Mundi," said Astra, "you can live with me and Alf and Mom and Dad. I know they'll like you. They'll probably be a little startled when they wake up and find there's a Nameless Horror aboard, but they'll soon get used to you, especially when I tell them about all the brave stuff you did."

It was hard to tell what the Nameless Horror was thinking at first, with his big, blank face like that of a weathered statue. But then his mouth curved upward at the corners, like a drawing of a smile. "I think I would like that," he said.

"There!" said Pilbeam, stepping back from the computer panel with self-satisfied lights blinking on and off all over his round body. And out of speakers set somewhere in the control room's walls came the big, warm, motherly voice of the ship itself.

"COURSE CORRECTION," it said, and the ship shook ever so slightly as it angled its nose toward the sun of Nova Mundi. "CORRECT HEADING RE-ESTABLISHED. ON COURSE FOR NOVA MUNDI. PASSENGERS SHOULD RETURN TO THEIR PODS."

"Do *you* need to hibernate?" asked Astra, looking up at the Nameless Horror.

He shook his head. "Ninety-nine years is a short time for me. I shall watch over you while you sleep, in case any other troubles befall the ship."

Astra and the Nameless Horror made one last journey to the dining hall and very carefully ordered a picnic for themselves from Nom-O-Tron. There was bread and jam, and cookies, and fruit, and strawberry milk, but there wasn't any cake because neither of them was in the mood for cake. They ate it in the

dappled light among the trees in the over-grown garden, while little e-bugs hummed about them, and Astra got to have almost all of it, because Earth food didn't really agree with the Nameless Horror. He crunched happily on the packaging instead.

Then Astra found some paper and a pen and wrote a note for the Nameless Horror that he could show to the grown-ups if they woke up before Astra did.

This is the Nameless Horror → He is **Brave** and **Kind** and saved the ship while you were sleeping. Please be friendly to him.   Love, Astra

She wrote a note to stick on the front of Nom-O-Tron as well, just in case anybody woke up feeling peckish and made the same mistake that she had.

She cleaned her teeth and brushed her hair, and Bedbot fussed busily around her as she went back to her pod. She didn't let the robot put her straight to sleep, though. First she went to the pods where her mom and dad and baby Alf lay and watched them sleeping for a while. "Sleep tight," she said. "See you on Nova Mundi, when the day is dawning."

Then she climbed into her own pod and snuggled down with Mammoth and her other cuddlies. The Nameless Horror smiled in at her as the lid closed, and Pilbeam said, "Sleep well, Astra."

"It's funny," said Astra. "You'd think I'd be tired after all those adventures, but I really don't feel . . . even . . . a . . . little . . . bit . . ."

Pilbeam and the Nameless Horror tiptoed quietly away.

* * *

The ship flew on, carrying its sleeping passengers across the dark light-years. Astra slept too, and all the dreams that came to her were happy ones. Pilbeam and the Nameless Horror looked in at her sometimes and checked that she was sleeping soundly, but she never stirred.

* * *

The next time she woke, the bright, golden light of a new sun was streaming through the ship's windows, and her mom was saying, "Wake up, Astra, you sleepyhead! We're here!"

Astra sat up. For a moment she thought, *What a strange dream I had!* Then she saw the Nameless Horror standing behind her parents, smiling down.

"Hello!" she said. "What's for breakfast?"

SARAH McINTYRE

IS SECRETLY AN ALIEN FIGHTER PILO[T] FROM THE PLANET POINTISPEX. ARRIVING ON EARTH WITH HER SPACE PENS AND A SUITCASE FULL OF HATS, SHE HAS USED HER SUPERIOR DRAWING SKILLS TO BECOME A LEADING ILLUSTRATOR AND COMICS ARTIST. HER SPACESHIP IS CURRENTLY PARKED IN SOUTH LONDON

PHILIP REEVE

WROTE HIS FIRST SPACE ADVENTURE AT THE AGE OF FIVE. HE CALLED IT "SPIKE AND SPOOK GO TO THE MOON" AND IT FEATURED AN ASTRONAUT AND HIS DOG. FEELING TERRIBLY PLEASED WITH HIMSELF, HE WENT ON TO WRITE MANY MORE STORIES. HE HAS MARKED OUT A LANDING SITE FOR PASSING SPACECRAFT IN HIS GARDEN ON DARTMOOR. HE HASN'T BEEN VISITED BY ALIENS YET (APART FROM SARAH) BUT HIS SPOONS HAVE MYSTERIOUSLY VANISHED.

The Poglites' costumes were designed by TIP TOP CHIMNEY POTS OF LYNMOUTH